I Want a Shop!

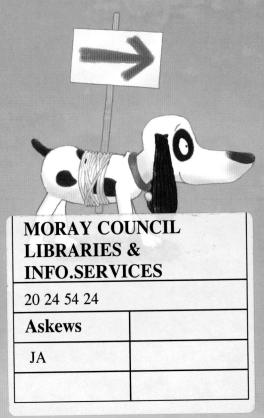

Licensed by The Illuminated Film Company
Based on the LITTLE PRINCESS animation series © The Illuminated Film Company 2008
Made under licence by Andersen Press Ltd., London
'I Want a Shop!' episode written by Dan Wicksman.
Producer Iain Harvey. Director Edward Foster.
© The Illuminated Film Company/Tony Ross 2008
Design and layout © Andersen Press Ltd, 2008.
Printed and bound in China by Midas Printing Ltd.
10   9   8   7   6   5   4   3   2   1
British Library Cataloguing in Publication Data available.

ISBN: 978 1 84270 762 3

This book has been printed on acid-free paper

I Want a Shop!

Tony Ross

Andersen Press · London

"Come on, slowcoaches!"
The Little Princess had been out shopping. The King and Queen slowly trudged behind her, loaded down with carrier bags.

"It must be all your truffles," huffed the King.

"It must be all your sprouts," puffed the Queen.

The Little Princess giggled and skipped ahead. "That was fun!"

Back at the castle, the Little Princess had a marvellous idea. "I'm going to have my own shop!" She raced up to her bedroom to find some things to sell.

The Little Princess rummaged in her toy box, then picked out a
dolly. "I can't sell that," she decided. "I might want to play with it."
She looked at everything, then put everything back.
"I need to find other things to sell instead."

The Little Princess pushed her pram along the castle corridor.

"What's this?"

She picked a wooden box off the table and gave it a shake.

A jack-in-the-box sprung out. "Ooohhh!" gasped the Little Princess. "I could sell this." As nobody was using the jack-in-the-box, she tossed it into the pram.

The castle was full of things
that nobody was using.
In the Gardener's shed, she
found three lovely pots.

In the Chef's kitchen
cupboards, she discovered
an interesting bowl with
holes in it.

The castle living room had even more treasures.

The Little Princess started with the King's old train set.

"He's too big to play with it now," she decided.

"There!" announced the Little Princess. "Lots of lovely stuff!"
She placed her teddy on the counter of her brand new shop.
"You can help me, Gilbert."

Her stall was finally ready, but where were the shoppers?
The Little Princess looked down at Scruff, then decided
to take action. "I've got a job for you."

"Woah, girl!" commanded the General, when he spotted Scruff's arrow. "Well, this looks jolly interesting."
He quickly re-mounted Nessie and cantered inside.

No one could resist the Little Princess's sign.
"Is it a treasure hunt?" grinned the Admiral, taking out his
telescope. Scruff wagged his tail and spun round. Standing still
is difficult for dogs.

The General pointed at the silver colander. "What's this?"

"Err…" paused the Little Princess. "It's a nice horsey hat for Nessie."

"I'll take it!" cried the General. "How much is it?"

The Little Princess
hadn't thought about paying.
"It's yours for a ride on Nessie."
The General beamed.
"It's a deal!"

"Look, Dad!" she called. "You can do a magic trick with these pots!" The King was so impressed, he bought the pots in exchange for promising to tell the Little Princess a story later.

"Princess!" frowned the Chef. " I do
not want to buy a choo choo train."
"But it will make things come to you,"
said the Little Princess.
She sent the salt and pepper
up the track and sold him
the train in seconds.

Scruff's sign tempted the Gardener in for a browse. "Do you
have anything to keep those pesky rabbits off my vegetables?"
The Little Princess reached for her jack-in-the-box.
"I've got just the thing."
"I'll take it!" chuckled the Gardener. "And I'll give you some
strawberries in return."

The Little Princess grinned. By the time she'd sold a windmill to the Prime Minister, her shop was nearly sold out.

"Hello!" called the Prime Minister, speeding outside on his trike.

The Gardener and the King looked very cross. "They're my plant pots!" shouted the Gardener. The King shook his head. "I bought this trick at the Princess's shop!"

The General trotted over, then suddenly pulled up in front of the Prime Minister. "That's my windmill!"

A queue of unhappy customers gathered outside the
Little Princess's shop.
The King stepped forward. "Did you take all these things?"

"But you never use them," argued the Little Princess.
"It doesn't mean you can go taking other people's things," frowned the King.
"OK," sighed the Little Princess. "Everyone swap back."

"Nobody likes my shop," sniffed the Little Princess.
Now she wouldn't get a ride on Nessie, a long story, a trike ride,
or any of the other things she had been promised!

Over the other side of the garden, the
Prime Minister did something very special.
"Gardener, you need this more than me."
The Gardener looked down at the
jack-in-the-box and beamed.

The Prime Minister's kind gesture gave the King an idea.
"Maybe we should all swap back?"
Everyone passed back their shopping, then set out to find
the Little Princess.

"We've decided that we should keep what we bought," explained the King. The Little Princess gasped.

"Really?"

"Yes," said the General. "So we've all come to pay you!"

The Little Princess's shop had earned her all sorts of wonderful treats. It had been an afternoon of stories, horse-play and trike rides.

"Princess!" sang the Chef. "We 'ave your cakes!"

"And your strawberries," added the Gardener.

"Yummy!" cheered the Little Princess. "But there are so many…"
Suddenly she burst into giggles.

"...I can sell them in my shop!"